The Tanzania Juma Stories

Juma and Little Sungura

by Lisa Maria Burgess

illustrated by Abdul M. Gugu

BARRANCA PRESS

Hello. My name is Juma.

I am Tanzanian. My *Baba* is from the island of Zanzibar and my *Mama* is from the mainland of Tanzania.

Like a little rabbit, I am super quick and full of tricks, so my parents call me **Super Sungura**.

But most of the time, I am just Juma—Ijumaa when *Mama* wants to be serious.

Guess what? When I was little, I didn't want to be just Juma. I wanted to be Juma and his brother or Juma and his sister. Guess what, what?

I needed a baby in my family.

My cousin Akida had a baby brother. His name was Mrefu.

At school, my friends Emmanuel and Pragya had babies in their families. When their mothers came to fetch them at the end of the day, I saw them.

Emmanuel had a baby sister named Miriam, and Pragya had a brother named Ananda.

Guess what? *Hakuna shida*—that means no worries. I had a good plan.

Guess what, what? I told *Mama* that I had a baby in my tummy. She laughed and said she had one in her tummy too.

I said mine was a baby sister—a *dada*. I told *Mama* that her baby was a brother—a *kaka*. Then I changed my mind. I had a baby in my tummy and it was a baby boy. I told *Mama* that her baby was a girl.

I just had one problem. My tummy was flat.

But *Mama*'s tummy was getting round, round, round.

I told *Baba* about my problem.

He laughed and said *Hakuna shida*. He put a big basketball under his shirt. He helped me put a football under my shirt. Our tummies looked round.

Baba asked, "Who has the biggest, roundest tummy?!"

Guess what? It was still *Mama*.

And she didn't put a ball under her dress.

One night I woke up. I thought I fell out of bed, but I was not on the floor. *Baba* was carrying me.

I told *Baba* I needed that bed. He said, "Tonight is special. You're having a sleepover with Akida."

Only, I didn't understand. Why go in the middle of the night? I liked to play all day and stay up all night—not drive somewhere in the dark and go straight to bed.

Guess what? That cousin Akida was already asleep and he isn't good at sharing. He's especially not good at sharing his bed.

Guess what, what? I was too sleepy to argue with *Baba*.

The next day I played the whole, whole day with Akida. It was a different kind of sleepover!

When *Baba* came to get me after his work at the bank, he drank tea. Then he said we had to check on *Mama*. Only, I didn't understand. She usually checked on me.

First we bought a *kanga*. Then we went to the hospital where I came out of *Mama*'s tummy. *Baba* said to wait on the bench. He went to find out where *Mama* and the baby were resting.

Then I understood—they don't call me *Super Sungura* for nothing. That baby got tired of growing and was ready to play—she came out of *Mama*'s tummy—same as I did—in the same hospital.

Guess what? I knew that baby would be bored in a hospital. That baby needed something fun.

There's nothing fun in a hospital except syringes, and the nurses don't share syringes with little boys; they're too dangerous. I know. I've asked.

I looked around. I remembered that the hospital is just across from the beach. *Hakuna shida.* I went out the door and crossed the road. I was careful. I looked both ways—right, left, right, left—all the way across to the trees.

Then I walked on the sand. I was lucky. The tide was low—that means the water has gone far away from the beach. I walked out on the flat land left by the tides and looked and looked until....

Guess what? I found a crab with lots of wiggly legs.

Guess what, what? I put that Mr. *Kaa* in my pocket.

I stood and watched a container ship until I heard *Baba* calling me with his big voice.

I explained to him in my small voice why we needed a crab. He kept talking in his big voice, "Don't you ever do that again. Don't go away without asking permission."

Finally he gave me a big hug and held my hand tight while we walked back to the hospital.

Mama's new *kanga* was crumpled from all that jumping and running. I said, *Hakuna shida. Mama* and that baby were sure to like Mr. *Kaa* lots, lots, lots more.

*M*ama was lying in a bed. She smiled at us and felt the crumpled *kanga*.

Then she pulled back a cover and I saw that baby. Only she was a lot smaller than Akida's baby or Emmanuel's baby or Pragya's baby. Our baby was tiny, tiny.

I tried to give her the crab, but she didn't want to open her eyes and Mr. *Kaa* just wanted to hide.

"Isn't your *dada* beautiful?" said *Mama*.

I said, "Yes, *Mama*," but I wasn't so sure at all. I never saw such a small, wrinkly baby!

Then *Mama* and that baby took a rest. So *Baba* and I returned Mr. *Kaa* to the beach.

Soon, *Baba* and I went back to the hospital and brought that baby and *Mama* home. *Baba* helped *Mama* unpack her bag.

This time, my baby opened her eyes and looked at me. I knew she was ready to play. I got my little black motorcycle. I zoomed around and showed my baby how it worked. Then I parked real close to the bed.

Careful, careful, I took her from the bed and put her on the motorcycle. Only she slid off. I told her, "*Little Sungura*, I can't push the motorcycle and hold you at the same time!"

Baba saw us. He looked at me with big round eyes, grabbed that baby, and shouted, "Are you a *Super Sungura* or what?"

I said, "Yes, *Baba*."

Many people visited. They brought food for *Mama* and presents for our baby. I opened the presents. Mostly they were not things I like—just diapers and bottles and frilly dresses.

I was also in charge of explaining: First the visitors asked, "What is her name?" I said, "We both get the name that *Baba* and *Babu* share. Then I have my special name: I am Ijumaa because I was born on a Friday. Her special name is Sareeya. She gets *Bibi*'s name because God brought her safe to us in the middle of the night. It was sooo dark that nobody could see, especially a wrinkly baby with her eyes closed."

Baba said I didn't need to explain that last part. Then they asked, "Who does Sareeya look like?" Some people said her eyes look like *Baba*'s eyes. Some people said she has *Mama*'s hands.

I said, "No way. My baby looks just like me! She is a Little Sungura."

And let me tell you... Now that she is getting bigger, I have plenty of super amazing plans for me and her....

Tanzania

Juma lives in Dar es Salaam in the east African country of Tanzania.

Tanzania stretches east to the beaches of the Zanzibar islands, west to the plains of the mainland, south to Lake Tanganyika, and north to Lake Victoria and the peak of Mount Kilimanjaro.

People in his family speak ki-Swahili and English, as well as ki-Sukuma and other languages. Juma likes to repeat words, which is a habit in ki-Swahili: In English we might say something like "very slow", but in ki-Swahili we would say *pole, pole* ("slow, slow").

Tanzania is famous for all sorts of wonderful things – the spices grown in Zanzibar, the coffee and tea grown in the highlands and the cotton in the lowlands, the purple, blue stone called Tanzanite found deep in the earth, and of course the wild animals that live in the national parks.

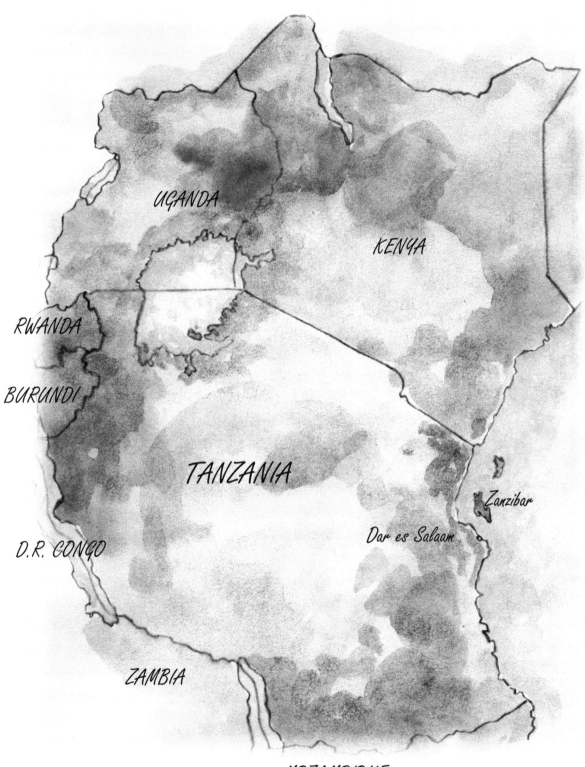

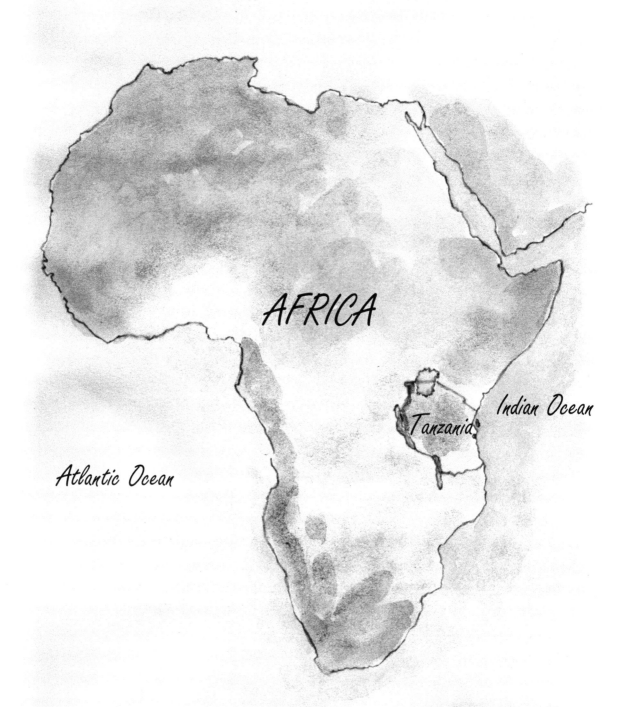

AFRICA

Tanzania

Indian Ocean

Atlantic Ocean

Juma's Family

Baba

Mama

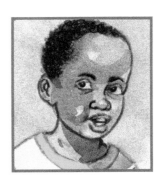

Juma
also known as
Super Sungura

Sareeya
also known as
Little Sungura

Ki-Swahili and English Glossary:

Baba:	Father
Babu:	Grandfather
Bibi:	Grandmother
Dada:	Sister
Hakuna shida:	No worries
Kaa:	Crab
Kaka:	Brother
Kanga:	Printed fabric used for skirts and scarves
Mama:	Mother
Sungura:	Rabbit

Names:

Akida:	officer, captain
Ijumaa:	born on a Friday
Mrefu:	tall and long
Sareeya:	night clouds

About the Authors:

At the time of writing these stories,
Lisa Maria Burgess taught in the
Department of Literature at the
University of Dar es Salaam. She
wrote the Juma stories with her sons,
Matoko and **Senafa**.

About the Illustrator:

Abdul M. Gugu lives in Dar es Salaam
where he works as an illustrator of
children's books and as an artist.

FIRST EDITION, July 2013

ISBN 978-1-939604-06-4

Library of Congress Control Number: 2013903967

Manufactured in the United States of America.

CPSIA information can be obtained
at www.ICGtesting.com
Printed in the USA
BVHW090659110620
581241BV00012B/291